CARL

the Chameleon Goes 2 school

DANIEL SWANSON
Illustrated by: Christina Streit

WRITING

231
x 2
462

SOCIAL STUDIES

200÷10=?

349
+50
399

3
4

ART

GYM

SCIENCE

Cc Aa Rr Ll

Carl

MUSIC

565
-25
540

READING

MATH

HISTORY

Aloha. I'm Carl, a Jackson chameleon from Kona on the Big Island of Hawaii. I live on Greenwell coffee farm. You won't believe what happened to me a few days ago. I was minding my own business, chillin' in the sun, taking in some warm rays. It felt so good. Too good, perhaps. I started feeling drowsy, my eyelids started to droop and I felt like I was drifting off into a nice, comfortable snooze.

ZZZZ...

Suddenly, I was jolted by the sound of my mother calling. " Get up Carl. It's time to go to school."

What? Go to School? I couldn't believe what I was hearing. "But mom, I'm just a chameleon. Why do I have to go to school?"

"I want you to grow up to be a smart chameleon," my mom answered, "and that means going to school. I'll fix you up a nice breakfast of juicy spiders and caterpillars so get ready to go."

I really had no choice. Mom rules. So after breakfast I began the walk towards the top of the macnut tree where the school was located.

Soon, there I was, sitting at my desk towards the back of the classroom, looking at the blackboard in front. Boooooring. Mrs. Shandler is our teacher and I'm quite sure she doesn't like me. Sometimes when I'm daydreaming she'll suddenly call on me to answer a question. How can I answer if I don't know what the question is? So unfair.

CES '14

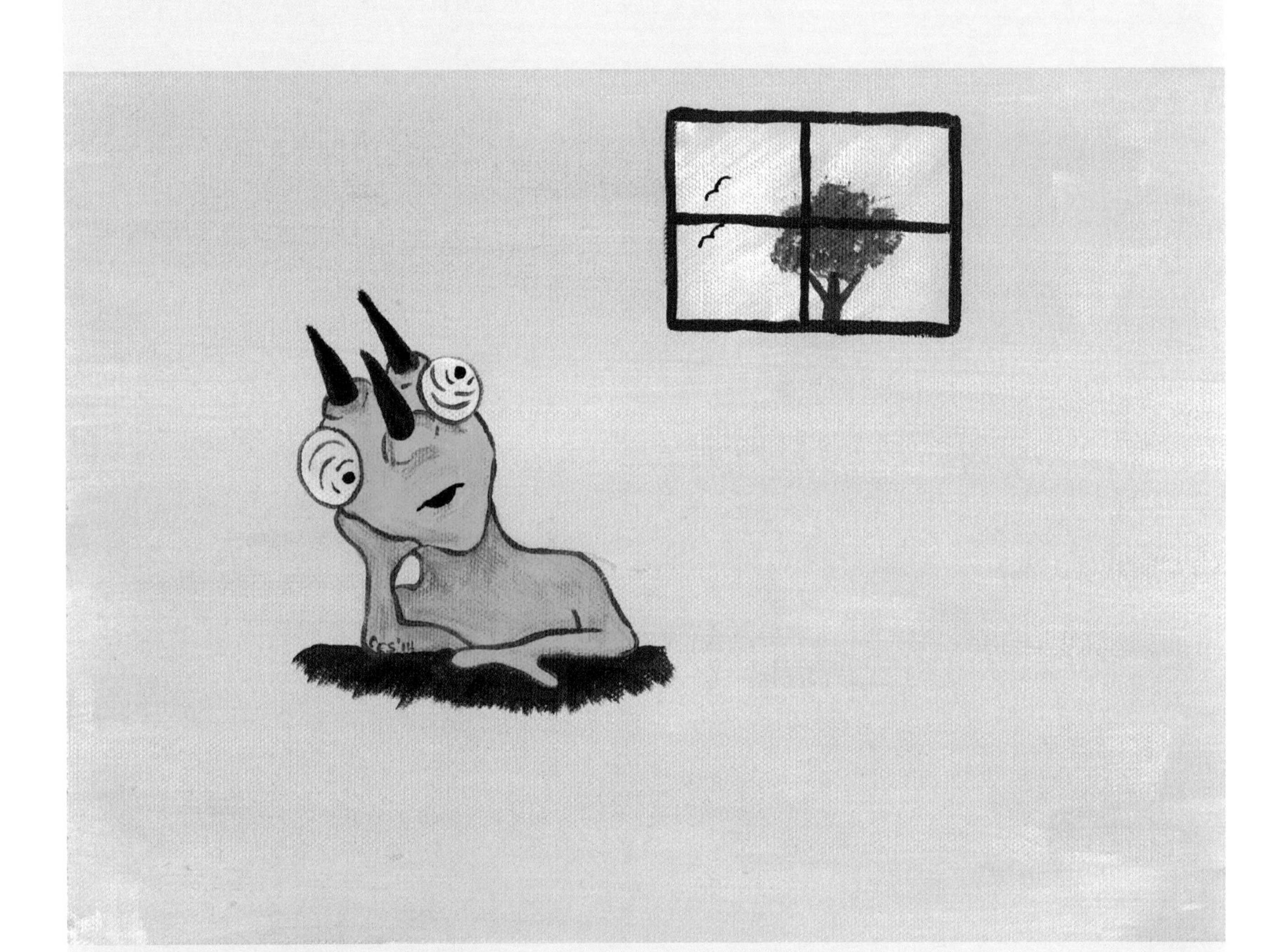

Since we chameleons have eyes that can move separately and look in different directions at the same time, my father told me I should always keep one eye focused on the teacher. Sounded like good advice so that's what I did. One eye was looking straight forward but the other one started to wander. I couldn't help it. I really couldn't.

Soon, my wandering eye spotted Chloe, sitting on the other side of the classroom. She's really cute and really nice. I wish I could be her special friend. I definitely needed to do something to impress her, get her attention. Unfortunately, sitting right behind her was Brax, the class bully. He's big, mean, and picks on other kids. My dad says I should stand up to bullies.

That's easy to say, not so easy to do.
He's like twice my size!
He could squish me like a spider
slammed by a rolled newspaper.
I wish all bullies would just disappear.

Brax spotted me looking at Chloe and then
suddenly stuck his tongue out towards me.
We chameleons have long tongues and
his came halfway across the classroom. Gross!
Of course, I had to respond so I did the same
thing back. Unfortunately, that was right when
Mrs. Shandler was glancing back from the
blackboard with one of her eyes.
Once again, I'm the one who got in trouble.

When class ended, Mrs. Shandler gave me a note she said I was to take home, have my parents sign and then bring back to her. Talk about stress. That's like going home and asking to be grounded. I decided to bury the note somewhere instead, hoping Mrs. Shandler would forget about it. Well, excuse me for living because it actually seemed like a good idea at the time.

To the
of

I was making my way towards home after school, a bit off the beaten path, looking for a place to bury the note. That's when I heard some noise, a commotion up ahead. I made my way around a rock, then a fallen papaya and suddenly, right there was Brax the bully picking on Chloe and some of her friends. I couldn't believe it.

It made me so mad I turned bright red, a color
we Jackson chameleons shouldn't be able to
turn. I was too mad to be scared and this was
my chance to be Chloe's hero.
It was now or never.

BAM

Yelling as loud as I could, I charged at Brax, pointing my three horns right at him. He stood there, frozen to the ground. Must have been surprised. BAM! I hit him so hard it was like an explosion. And then I started shaking and shaking.

And shaking some more, I suddenly heard my mother's voice. "Carl, wake up. You've been dreaming. Were you having a nightmare?"

"What? Dreaming? Sleeping?" My mind was a fog. "You mean, mom, I wasn't at school?"

"School?" my mom said. "You silly boy. You're a chameleon. You don't go to school. Only humans do that. Now go out and hunt for some bugs and make yourself useful."

"Wow, mom. You're the best. Thanks."

"Oh, by the way Carl, while you were napping, a girl stopped by and left you a note. I think her name was Chloe."

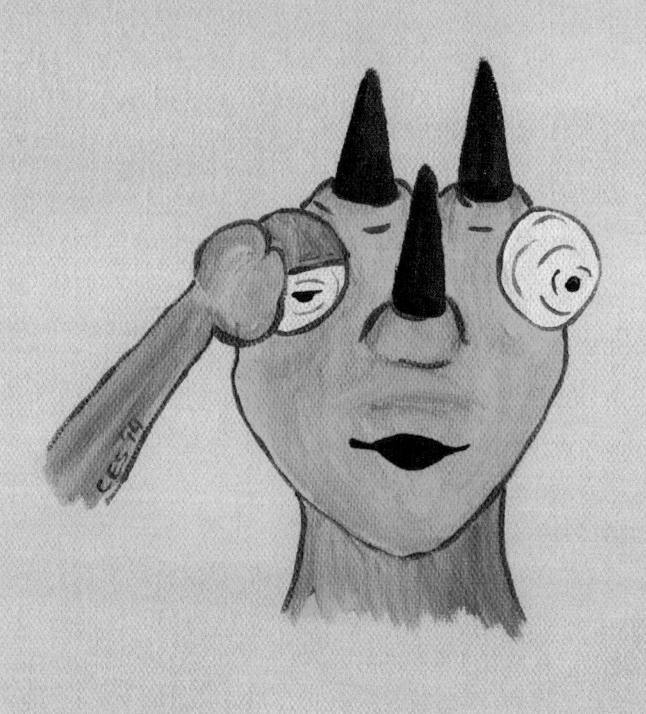

Love
Chloe

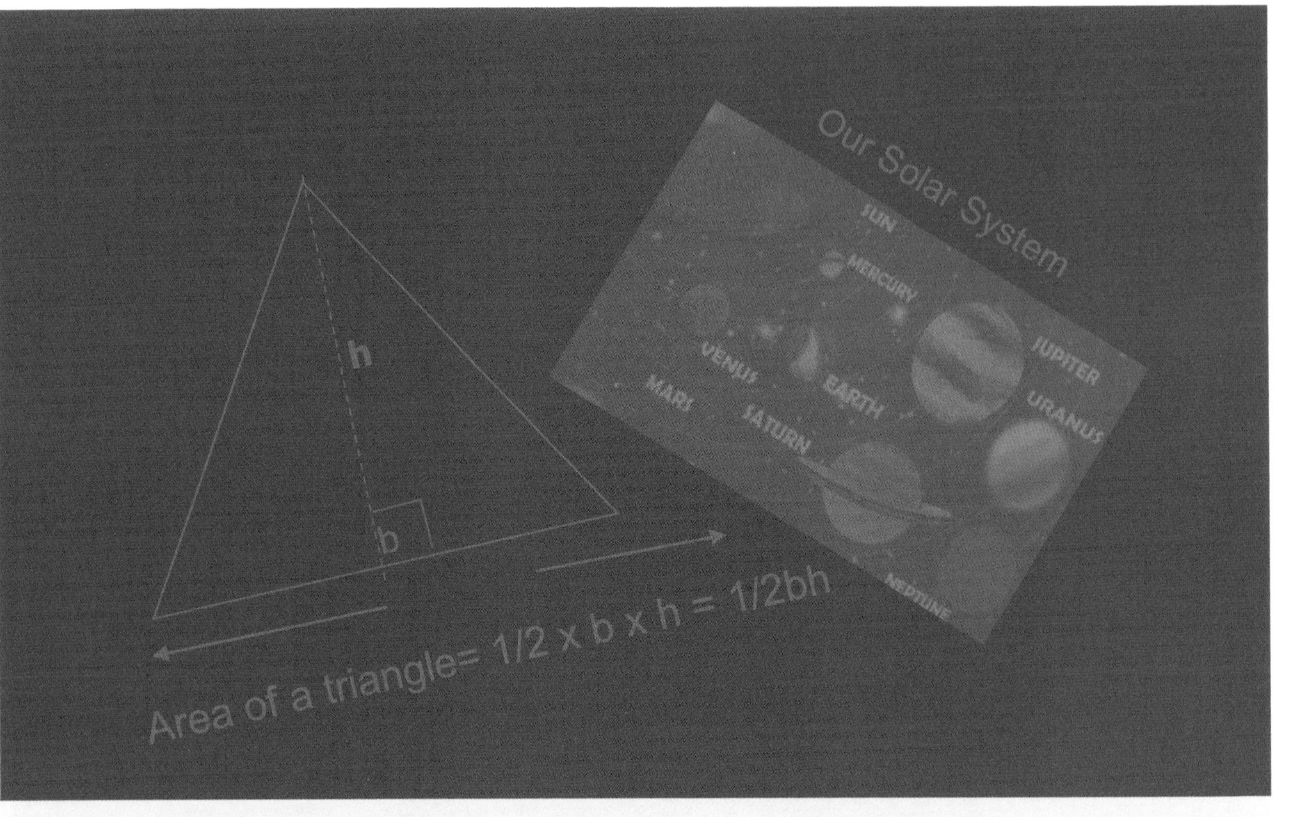
Our Solar System
SUN
MERCURY
VENUS
JUPITER
MARS
EARTH
URANUS
SATURN
NEPTUNE
h
b
Area of a triangle= 1/2 x b x h = 1/2bh

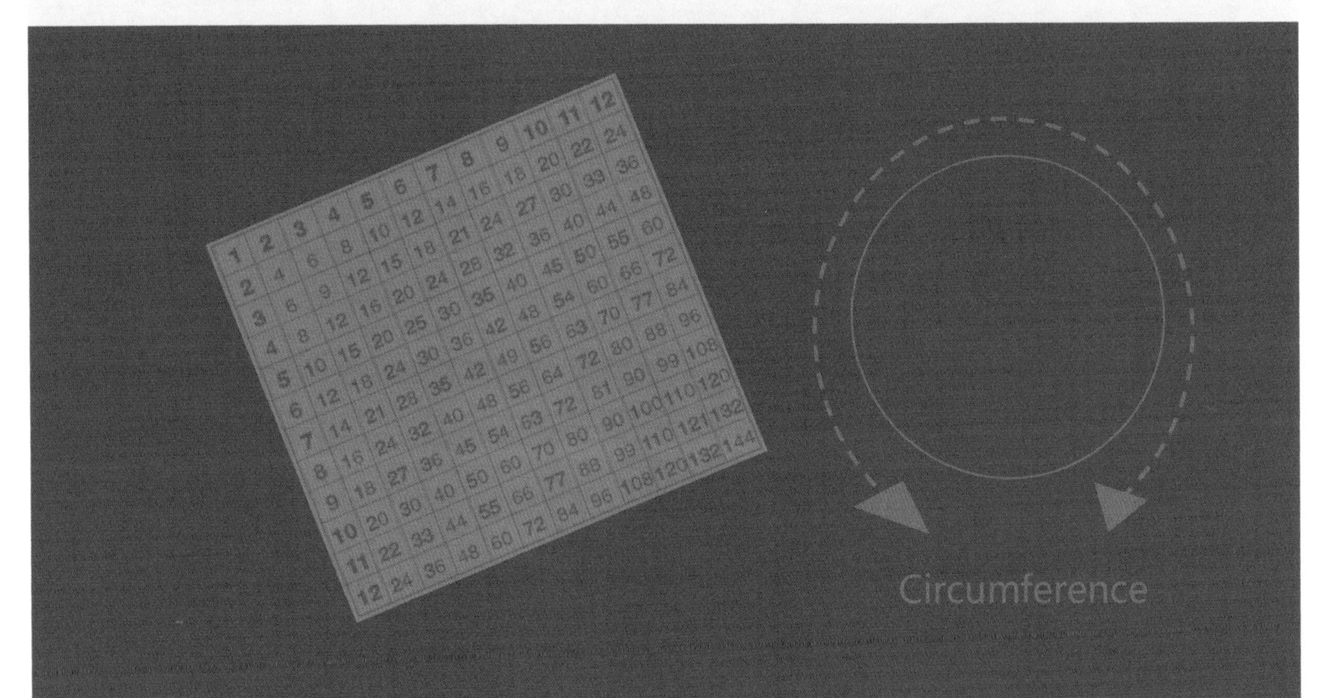
Circumference

Five Fun facts about chameleons

**Get your pencil ready kids!
It's time to take my quiz.
Test your knowledge about other chameleons who are just like me.**

Directions: Circle True or False.

1. **Is a chameleons tongue twice the length of its body?**

   True or False

2. **Do the eyes of a chameleon move separately?**

   True or False

3. **Do Jackson chameleons give live birth and not lay eggs?**

   True or False

4. **Is the life span of a Jackson chameleon an average up to 6 years?**

   True or False

5. **Does a male chameleon have three horns and a female have none?**

   True or False

Answer key: Questions 1 through 5 are all True. If you marked True for all five questions you scored 100%.
Good Job! For completing the test you get a gold star. ☆

Made in the USA
Charleston, SC
09 June 2016